*Dedicated to my loving wife, Sue
and the day we had lunch together
at Cracker Barrel in Waco, Texas –
where I discovered this photo
and the idea for this story.*

~ FRAN FOUND ME~

It was another Friday as Francis Conley and I were returning from lunch to our desk jobs at the R.B. Rutherford Business Building in downtown Dallas, Texas. As was often the case, Fran and I - if we had the time, would do a little sightseeing and shop at the stores along our way.

This particular day we found ourselves looking at some things in the big antique store on Elm Street. All of a sudden, Fran, who had been looking at some things at the other end of the store, came running up to me, shouting, "Doris! Doris! I found you!"

"Of course you have," I replied. "Now, let's get back to the office."

"NO! Come see – just take a look for yourself!" Fran exclaimed.

"What on earth are you talking about?" I said as Fran was pulling on me to come to a table of old pictures where she had been rummaging around.

She then began pointing at a picture of a young girl wearing a cap and gown with a diploma in her hand.

By now, I understood the urgency. It was me. This graduation picture did look exactly like me. I couldn't believe my eyes, but all I said was, "Well, they do say that each of us has a twin, and this one is mine."

"Maybe so," Fran says, "but can you believe this? Maybe it's a long lost relative or something."

"Well, that's possible. I guess, but I'm adopted, you know." I claimed, as I found myself shying away from the picture.

"No, you never told me you were adopted." Fran holds out her arms as to try and hug me as if the adoption left me scarred and forever desiring hugs.

I went on to explain that even though she and I had become the best of friends over the last few years, there are probably many things about our lives that we have never shared. Fran agrees but talks me into buying the picture and at a bargain price of four dollars.

I didn't care about knowing who I was.

I was adopted as a baby by John and Marie Harris – the most loving and caring parents a girl could hope for, so wondering all these years if a biological parent was out there never mattered that much to me. The Harris family was all I ever needed or wanted.

Fran and I, and the picture, made our way back to work early this Friday afternoon. I took the framed print back to my apartment that evening, left it sitting on a shelf in my living room, and that's where it stayed for several weeks.

~

Many weekends I forego cleaning my apartment until it becomes unbearable, and I must.

I was in the organizing and cleaning mode for some reason, and I picked up the picture of my twin and began to rub the dust off. Not even thinking, I carefully proceeded to pull the back cover and stand away from the picture to clean the frame and glass. As I pulled, the back of the photo itself began to tear off like strips of old, thin wallpaper.

On this brown cardboard-like backing was the neatest handwriting I had ever seen.

Lorene Landrum
Tulsa, Oklahoma

I didn't give it much thought, but I didn't forget about it either. I knew what I had been saying, "Everyone has a twin", but did I believe that?

Could this person possibly be my real biological mother?

~

Later that summer, it was time for me to take a much-needed vacation from work, and if I didn't use it – I would lose it. Having already visited my family numerous times throughout the year, I decided to go to Oklahoma to Tulsa. The thought was spinning in my head like a Ferris wheel that never stopped, continually moving, never letting anyone on or off.

I kept asking myself if I was about to turn over or dig up stones that I shouldn't? Should I just leave it alone? Maybe even throw the picture away?

Fran was thrilled that I was going and kept reassuring me it was the right thing to do.

She even went to the boss to ask for vacation days, but that didn't work since we do the same job and are always filling in for one another.

July 1, 1965 – I boarded a Greyhound bus at the Dallas Terminal and headed out to Tulsa.

Not knowing what I was about to find or lose, I was a tad bit excited.

Once arriving in Tulsa, I got off the bus and waved a taxi over. Once in the car, I ask him to take me to a nice hotel – any hotel he recommends. I hadn't made any reservations, as to stay spontaneous and keep up the theme of my adventure. The taxi driver seemed to know exactly where I should stay. He looked like such a good, dependable man, but he could be a serial killer for all I knew.

There is a part of me that thought what I was doing was dangerous and careless, but that same part of me felt inspired.

The first night in my nice hotel room, I took the Tulsa phone book from the little nightstand, moving over the small Gideon Bible to find it. I began thumbing through the pages and looking for the name Landrum. There was no Lorene Landrum, as was written on the back of the picture, but there were several Landrums - both men and women. I wondered if Lorene was related to any of them.

I reached over to the phone on the same nightstand and just began dialing. I went through the list fairly quickly, "Hello, sorry to bother you, but I'm looking for a Lorene Landrum. Maybe you might know of her?" I was getting the same answer, "No, sorry honey; I haven't heard of her." I was nearing the end of my list, when I dialed the number for an Oleta Landrum, already thinking this was another dud of a call.

This call was different. After giving my usual spill, there was a longer than usual hesitation before this Oleta answered me. She said, "Yes, well, my husband's brother was Leroy Landrum, and he was married to Lorene."

My heart skipped a beat. I thought, could this be happening?

I ask, "Do you know where Leroy Landrum is living?"

"We buried him a year ago," Oleta answers. "and Lorene died a year before Leroy."

My questions stream without hesitation, "Did they have any children?"

I understood that Oleta had just told me they were both dead, but my inquiry continued without emotion, only hard-core persistence. I wanted to know the truth – where I came from. I could do that weird grieving-over-someone-I-never-knew stuff later.

"Only a daughter, Janelle, who now lives here in North Tulsa."

"Oh my," I didn't realize how nervous, and abrupt, my questions were coming across.

All of a sudden, Oleta asks, "Who are you, ma'am?"

What a question - I wasn't even prepared to answer that to myself, much less a stranger on the telephone. I knew my name was Doris, but today that seemed to be all I knew.

"Ma'am, I do believe that I am Lorene Landrum's daughter."

"No, you're not! Leroy and Lorene only had one daughter, and her name is like I've told you before, Janelle."

Oleta seems to be getting agitated and confused. Oleta and the family had never known of a child that Lorene had given birth to before she met and married Leroy. Somehow, I had convinced myself that I was Lorene's daughter, and I wouldn't take no for an answer. These feelings hid inside of me until this particular phone call, and they burst open like fireworks.

I calmed myself down and asked Oleta if she could get Janelle and me to meet with her and talk.

"I don't know, we'll see. I'll call you back tomorrow, okay?" She replies.

"Yes, and thank you," I said as I hung up the phone.

That night in the hotel was the longest and loneliest night of my life, or that I could remember. I stayed in my room the entire next day, not wanting to miss a phone call. Finally, at around 2:30, the phone rings!

I jerked the receiver and answered, "Hello?"

"Yes, this is Mrs. Oleta Landrum. Do you still want to meet with Janelle?"

"Of course!"

"Okay, we can meet at this small park, it's just north of Tulsa by the big Tulsa bus terminal. You'll see it. About five, if that's alright?"

"Sure, see you then. Uh, Oleta – I sure do thank you." We both hung up the phone.

It was almost five o'clock that evening as I walked back past the bus station. You could see the little park that

Oleta told me of and a short walkway that went down its center where there were some benches and tables. On one of the benches sat two women. As I approached them, the older lady, Oleta, stood up and calmly said, "Hello, you are Doris?"

"Yes," I answered immediately.

The other lady, who was quite a bit younger, also stood up and introduced herself, "Hello, I'm Janelle."

She certainly favored the graduation picture from the antique store. We all sat down, and Oleta just blurted out - "Okay, Doris. What exactly do you want to tell us?"

"Well, here goes." I took a deep breath in and let it out before I continued. I looked at Janelle and said, "I believe you and I are sisters, maybe half-sisters. I think we had the same mother, Lorene."

"Oh no! You don't know what you're saying. I am mother and daddy's only child. Aunt Oleta, I'm ready to leave." She grabs her purse and stands up.

I reach in my purse and pull out my photo of Lorene and hand it to them.

"You mean my mother, Lorene, had a baby way back before she ever met and married daddy and she never told anyone about it? I can't believe it! I won't."

"Oh my goodness," Oleta says.

No one said a word for what seemed to be an eternity. Oleta and Janelle just kept looking back into the park and then back to one another with confused and puzzled faces. Finally, Aunt Oleta speaks up so intelligently and in control.

"Okay, one of my best friends here in town works at the lab inside Franklin Hospital where they do paternity DNA examinations. I think they can do a sibling test, too. I can call her, set up a time, and get back with both of you." she looked at both of us for an agreement.

"Okay," I said.

"Well, okay," Janelle agrees.

Oleta comforts both of us, "I'll try and leave it all up to you girls. I'll get it set up, and you can each decide what you want to do."

Janelle, Oleta, and I are all in agreement as we leave the park.

A few days later, we go in for our appointment.

A few months later, I get a phone call from the hospital lab. It is positive. I am Janelle's sister and Lorene's daughter.

~

Life goes on for Janelle in Tulsa and me in Dallas. We would see each other a few times as the years pass, meeting some during holidays, and even introducing our families.

The past had left out a piece in my life's puzzle, and I didn't realize how important that part was until Fran found me.

CPSIA information can be obtained
at www.ICGtesting.com
Printed in the USA
LVHW110817260720
661548LV00011B/116

9 780578 688855